D1498220

First Facts™

Why in the World?

Why Do Birds Sing?

A Book about Animal Communication

by June Preszler

Consultant:
Dr. Bernd Heinrich
Department of Biology
University of Vermont

Capstone
press®
Mankato, Minnesota

First Facts is published by Capstone Press,
151 Good Counsel Drive, P.O. Box 669, Mankato, Minnesota 56002.
www.capstonepress.com

Library of Congress Cataloging-in-Publication Data
Preszler, June, 1954–
    Why do birds sing? : a book about animal communication / by June Preszler.
      p. cm.—(First facts. Why in the world?)
    Summary: "A brief explanation of animal communication, including how animals
communicate and why they need to"—Provided by publisher.
    Includes bibliographical references and index.
    ISBN-13: 978-0-7368-6756-6 (hardcover)
    ISBN-10: 0-7368-6756-2 (hardcover)
    1. Animal communication—Juvenile literature. I. Title. II. Series.
QL776.P734 2007
591.59—dc22   2006021445

Editorial Credits
Jennifer Besel, editor; Juliette Peters, set designer; Renée Doyle, book designer; Wanda Winch,
    photo researcher/photo editor

Photo Credits
Getty Images Inc./The Image Bank/Peter Dazeley, 18; Stone/Renee Lynn, 21;
    Taxi/Gary Randall, 7 (top left)
Index Stock Imagery/Steven Emery, 13
iStockphoto Inc./cjmckendry, cover (bird)
Minden Pictures/Flip Nicklin, 7 (bottom); Frans Lanting, 20; Mark Raycroft, 12;
    Stephen Dalton, 8, 16
Peter Arnold/Mike Powles, 15
Ron Kimball Stock/Ron Kimball, cover (chimp)
Seapics.com/Doug Perrine, 7 (top right); Larry Mishkar, 9
Shutterstock/Hiroyuki Saita, 5; Michael West, 10; Stefan Ekernas, 4
SuperStock/age fotostock, 17

413 2925

Table of Contents

Can Animals Talk?

Listen to birds sing. Watch honey bees dance. Animals don't use words to talk. But they do **communicate** in other ways. Communication helps animals find each other, get food, and stay safe.

Scientific Inquiry

Asking questions and making observations like the ones in this book are how scientists begin their research. They follow a process known as scientific inquiry.

Ask a Question

Why do dogs bark?

Investigate

Watch a dog for a day. In a notebook, write down when the dog barked. Make sure to note what was going on. Was there another dog nearby? Was the dog sitting by its dish or by the door? Finally, read this book to learn about animal communication.

Explain

You noticed that the dog barked when it needed to go outside. You also saw that the dog barked when other animals were near. You decide that dogs bark to communicate what they want or need. Write this down in your notebook and remember to keep asking questions.

5

How Do Animals Communicate?

An angry gorilla might stick out his tongue. Marine slugs make a stinky acid that tells **predators** to stay away. Whales sing songs to each other. Other animals receive these messages by using their **senses** of smell, sound, sight, or touch.

? Did You Know?
Kangaroos and rabbits thump their hind legs on the ground when danger is near. The sound warns others to stay away.

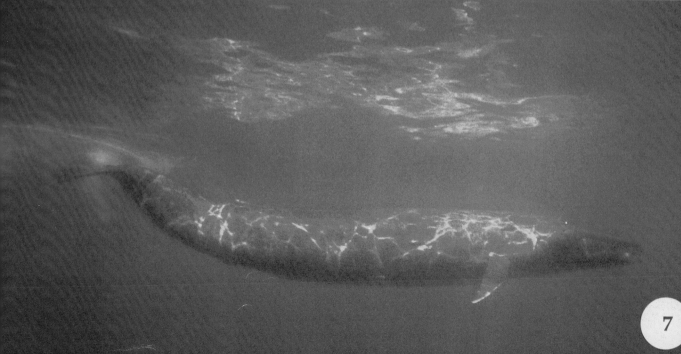

What Does Smell Tell?

A female moth flutters in the air.
Soon, her scent attracts male moths.
Her scent tells them she's ready
to **mate**.

Other animals release scents that act as warnings. A hurt fish produces an **odor** that warns other fish to stay away from a dangerous area.

Why Do Birds Sing?

Bird songs greet us as we wake. Birds aren't talking to us, though. They are telling other birds, "This is my place."

In spring, the male red-winged blackbird claims a home. He sings a song that tells other male birds to stay away. Later, he sings a new song that attracts a female.

Birds aren't the only creatures to use sound. Many animals use sound to find mates. The male elk makes a loud roar, telling females to stay near him.

Some animals make sounds with their wings. When a female mosquito flies, her wings make a high humming sound. The sound helps male mosquitoes find her, even in the dark.

? Did You Know?
Penguin parents call out to their chicks. The parent can hear its chick's answer among thousands of other chicks.

Why Do Monkeys Frown?

Some animals make faces and **gestures**. This body language sends messages that other animals can see. Rhesus monkeys are big frowners when they are worried. Monkeys also flutter their eyelids to show friendliness.

Other animals use their whole bodies to send messages. Honey bees dance to tell other bees they have found nectar.

? Did You Know?
Male fiddle crabs greet female fiddle crabs by waving their giant claws.

How Do Animals Talk with Touch?

Some animals communicate through touch. Bees can't see in their dark hives. They touch antennas to give messages to each other.

Touch can also show **affection** and caring. Monkeys take care of one another by picking lice and ticks out of each other's fur.

Can My Pet Talk to Me?

Pets send their owners many messages. Your dog might sit by his bowl to tell you he's hungry. Your cat might meow and rub against your leg to tell you she wants attention.

Whether the animals are pets or living in the wild, they communicate. Animals communicate to get what they need to survive in their surroundings.

CAN YOU BELIEVE IT?

Elephants are big animals and big talkers. Elephants communicate with each other by making close to 70 different sounds. And many of these sounds are so low, humans can't hear them. Scientists think that some of these really low sounds can be heard by other elephants at least 2.5 miles (4 kilometers) away!

Some scientists say people and animals communicate in similar ways. Just like people, apes and monkeys greet each other with kisses or by touching hands. In what other ways are human and animal communication the same?

21

GLOSSARY

affection (uh-FEK-shuhn)—a great liking for someone or something

communicate (kuh-MYOO-nuh-kate)—to share thoughts, feelings, or information

gesture (JESS-chur)—a movement that communicates a feeling or an idea

mate (MATE)—to join together to produce young; a mate is also the male or female partner of a pair of animals.

odor (OH-dur)—a smell

predator (PRED-uh-tur)—an animal that hunts other animals for food

sense (SENSS)—a way of knowing about your surroundings; hearing, smelling, touching, tasting, and sight are the five senses.

READ MORE

Ganeri, Anita. *Animal Communication.* Nature Files. Philadelphia: Chelsea House, 2005.

Niz, Xavier. *Animals Communicating.* Animal Behavior. Mankato, Minn.: Capstone Press, 2005.

Tatham, Betty. *How Animals Communicate.* Watts Library. New York: Franklin Watts, 2004.

INTERNET SITES

FactHound offers a safe, fun way to find Internet sites related to this book. All of the sites on FactHound have been researched by our staff.

Here's how:

1. Visit *www.facthound.com*

2. Choose your grade level.

3. Type in this book ID **0736867562** for age-appropriate sites. You may also browse subjects by clicking on letters, or by clicking on pictures and words.

4. Click on the **Fetch It** button.

FactHound will fetch the best sites for you!

INDEX